This Igloo book belongs to:

. . . .

. . . .

Reading Together

This story is written in a special way so that a child and an adult can 'take turns' in reading the text.

Firstly, it is always helpful to read the whole book to your child, stopping to talk about the pictures. Explain that you are going to read it again but this time the child can join in.

Read the left hand page and when you come to the sentence which is repeated on the other page run your finger under this. Your child then tries to read the same sentence opposite.

Searching for the child's sentence in the adult version is a useful activity. Your child will have a real sense of achievement when all the sentences on the right hand page can be read. Giving lots of praise is very important.

Enjoy the story together.

I Can Read...

Sleeping Beauty

Once upon a time a King and Queen were very happy. They were happy because they had a new baby girl.
"Let us have a party for our new baby," said the Queen.
"We can invite the fairies to the party," said the King.

"We can invite the fairies to the party," said the King.

It was the day of the party. The good fairies gave presents to the baby Princess.
"The Princess will be kind," said the first fairy.
"The Princess will be clever," said the second fairy.
"The Princess will be happy," said the third fairy.
The good fairies waved their magic wands.

The good fairies waved their magic wands.

Then a bad fairy came to the party.
"The Princess will die" said the bad fairy. The King's guards chased the bad fairy away. But it was too late.

Then a bad fairy came to the party.

"Please help my baby," said the Queen.
"I can help," said the fourth fairy.
"The baby will not die. But one day
she will prick her finger on a spinning
wheel. When she does this, she will fall
fast asleep for a hundred years."
The King and Queen threw away all the
spinning wheels in the palace.

“Please help my baby,”
said the Queen.

The baby Princess grew up.
She was kind and clever and happy.
But one day the Princess found a
spinning wheel.
She played with the spinning wheel.
"Ouch," said the Princess. "I have hurt
my finger!"

But one day the Princess found
a spinning wheel.

The Princess fell fast asleep.
The King and Queen fell asleep.
The guards and servants fell asleep.
Even the dogs and cats and mice
fell asleep.
Everyone in the palace fell asleep.

The Princess fell fast asleep.

The Princess slept for a hundred years.
Everyone in the palace slept for
a hundred years.
Thorns grew up all around the palace.
One day a brave Prince was out riding
near the palace.
He cut all the thorns down.

The Princess slept for
a hundred years.

The Prince went into the palace.
He went past the sleeping King and Queen.
He went past the sleeping guards and servants.

The Prince went into the palace.

At last the Prince found the sleeping Princess.
The Prince kissed the Princess.
The Princess woke up!

The Prince kissed the Princess.

The Prince and Princess fell in love. They got married and lived happily ever after in the palace.

The Prince and Princess fell in love.

Key Words

Can you read these words and find them in the book?

fairy

spinning wheel

King

Prince

Princess

Questions and Answers

Now that you've read the story can you answer these questions?

a. Who did the King invite to the party?

b. What did the Princess hurt her finger with?

c. Who kissed the Princess?

a. The fairies   b. Spinning wheel   c. The Prince

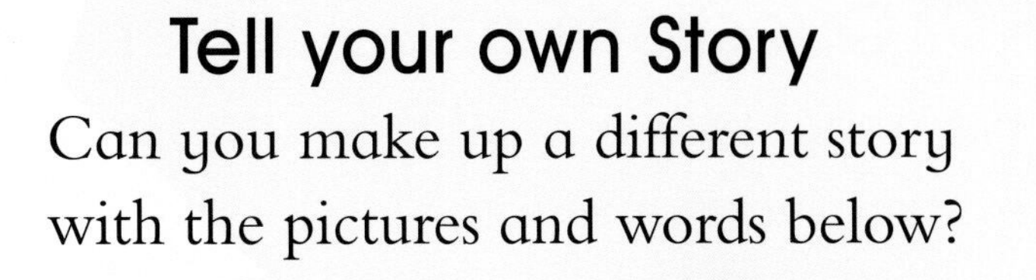

Tell your own Story

Can you make up a different story with the pictures and words below?

magic wand

Prince

King

spinning wheel

fairy
baby
cat
castle

Mix and Match

Draw a line from the pictures to the correct word to match them up.

fairy

castle

magic wand

spinning wheel

Prince

cat